NICKELODEON

WONDER PETS!

The Baby Bird Rescue!

adapted by Sascha Paladino
based on the screenplay "Save the What?" written by Sascha Paladino
illustrated by Todd McArthur, Little Airplane Productions

Simon Spotlight/Nickelodeon
New York   London   Toronto   Sydney

Based on the TV series *Wonder Pets!*™ as seen on Nickelodeon®

SIMON SPOTLIGHT

An imprint of Simon & Schuster Children's Publishing Division

1230 Avenue of the Americas, New York, New York 10020

For information about special discounts for bulk purchases, please contact Simon & Schuster Special Sales at 1-866-506-1949 or business@simonandschuster.com.

Manufactured in the United States of America 0110 LAK

First Edition 10 9 8 7 6 5 4 3 2 1

ISBN 978-1-4169-9077-2

Ring-ring-CLANG! Ring-ring-CLANG!
The red tin-can phone is ringing—but it doesn't sound right!

The Wonder Pets put on their hats and rush to answer the phone.

"It looks like someone needs help right in our backyard," says Linny. "But it's hard to see. There's something wrong with the phone!"

"Oh, no!" groan Tuck and Ming-Ming.

The phone is broken!

"Wow, this is going to be hard," says Ming-Ming.

"It sure is, Wonder Pets," says Linny. "We're going to need a bigger team today. Maybe you can help us! Will you be a Wonder Pet? Great!"

The Wonder Pets jump into the fabric scrap box and put on their superhero outfits!

"Since you're a Wonder Pet today, you need a cape too!" says Linny. "Here you go."

"Linny, Tuck, and Ming-Ming too!
We're Wonder Pets and so are you!"

"Let's bring the tin-can phone," says Ming-Ming, "in case it starts working again."

"Great idea!" says Linny, as Ming-Ming pulls the tin-can phone out of its socket. *Pop!*

The Wonder Pets work together to build the Flyboat!

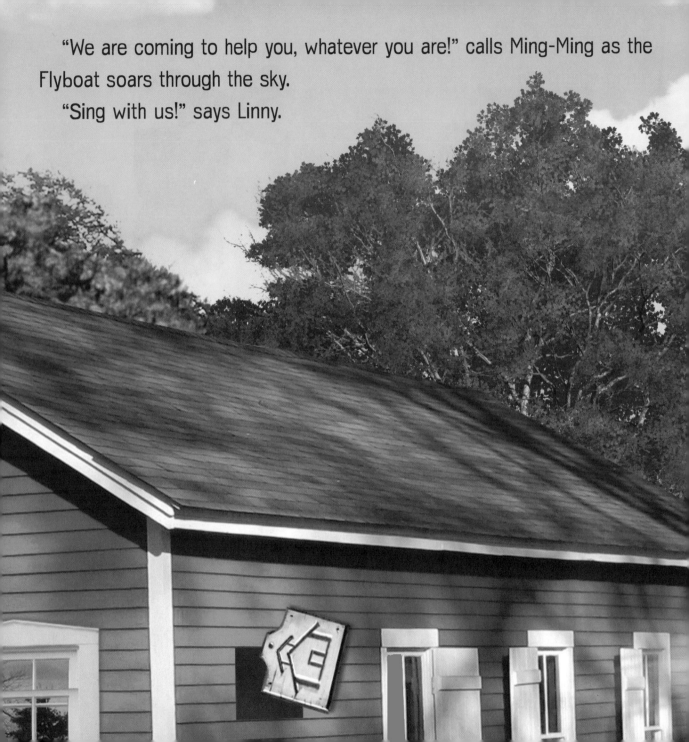

"We are coming to help you, whatever you are!" calls Ming-Ming as the Flyboat soars through the sky.

"Sing with us!" says Linny.

"Wonder Pets! Wonder Pets! We're on our way
to help a who-knows-what, and save the day!
We're not too big, and we're not too tough.
But when we work together, we've got the right stuff!
Go, Wonder Pets! Yay!"

As the Wonder Pets land in the backyard, the tin-can phone starts to ring again. *Ring-ring-CLANG!*

"Ooh!" says Ming-Ming. "Maybe if we look into the phone, we'll see another clue!"

The Wonder Pets look into the phone and see an apple tree.

"So," says Tuck, "the animal in trouble is near an apple tree."

"We need *your* help!" Linny says. "Do you see a tree that looks like the picture inside the phone? Yeah, there's an apple tree right there!"

"Apple-solutely!" says Ming-Ming.

"You're doing great, teammate!" says Linny.

As the Wonder Pets head toward the apple tree, the tin-can phone starts to ring again. *Ring-ring-CLANG!*

Together they look into the phone for another clue.

"I see feathery wings!" says Linny.

"And I see a beak!" says Tuck.

"Hmm," says Ming-Ming. "I wonder what it could be."

"We need *your* help, New Wonder Pet!" says Tuck. "What kind of animal has feathery wings and a beak? That's right! A bird!"

"Oh, yeah!" says Ming-Ming. "Now why didn't I think of that?"

"So, the animal in trouble is a bird!" says Linny. "Let's go find her!"

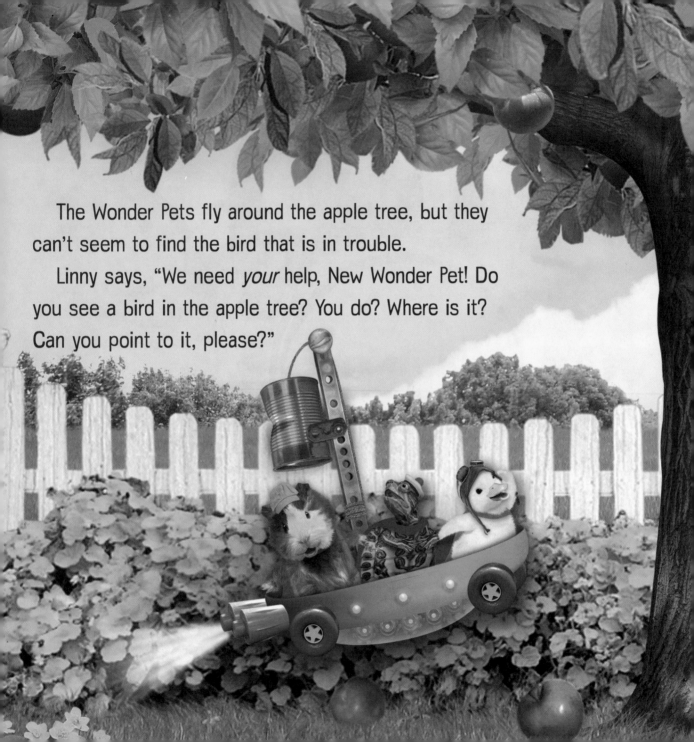

The Wonder Pets fly around the apple tree, but they can't seem to find the bird that is in trouble.

Linny says, "We need *your* help, New Wonder Pet! Do you see a bird in the apple tree? You do? Where is it? Can you point to it, please?"

The Wonder Pets look around and see a baby hummingbird with her beak stuck in an apple!

"Oh!" Linny says. "You found the animal in trouble! It's a baby hummingbird! When hummingbirds fly, their wings make a humming sound."

"Oh, no!" says Tuck. "The baby hummingbird's really stuck, and that apple is going to fall!"

"This is serious!" says Ming-Ming.

"We have to think of a way to save her—fast!" Linny shouts.

Hmm-hmm-hmmmmm! The baby hummingbird flaps her wings even harder.

"I know how we can save the baby hummingbird," says Ming-Ming.
"We can pull her out!"

"Great idea, Ming-Ming!" cheers Linny.

"We need someone really strong to help us pull the baby hummingbird out," says Linny. "Can *you* show us how *you* pull? Wow! Nice pulling. Now let's all pull together!"

As the Wonder Pets start to pull the baby
hummingbird, they begin to sing:
"What's going to work? Teamwork!
What's going to work? Teamwork!
Pull! Pull! Pull!"

Pop! The baby hummingbird pops out of the apple and into the Flyboat!
"Great pulling!" says Linny. "We did it!"
"And just in time!" says Tuck, as the apple falls to the ground.

Hmmm-hmmm-hmmmmm! The baby hummingbird flies away, flapping her wings happily.

Here's Papa Hummingbird!

"Thank you, Wonder Pets!" he says. "You saved my baby!"

"This calls for some celery!" cheers Linny.

"Have a slice of apple," offers Papa Hummingbird.

"Thanks! We can all have celery with apple," says Linny. "Here's some for *you*!"

"Yum," says Ming-Ming. "Celery and an apple slice—how nice!"

"Thank you for all your help today!" says Linny.

"We couldn't have done it without you," agrees Tuck.

"Yeah," says Ming-Ming. "It's been a dream having you on the team!"

The Wonder Pets are so happy that you helped them out today. You were a wonderful Wonder Pet!